Mama and Little Joe

For Emilia
— A. McA.

For Niki and Jude, with love
— T. M.

Margaret K. McElderry Books

An imprint of Simon & Schuster Children's Publishing Division

1230 Avenue of the Americas, New York, New York 10020

Text copyright © 2005 by Angela McAllister

Illustrations copyright © 2005 by Terry Milne

Originally published in Great Britain in 2005 by Simon & Schuster UK Ltd.

First U.S. edition, 2007

Published by arrangement with Simon & Schuster UK Ltd.

The text for this book is set in Joanna and Bernhard Modern.

The illustrations for this book are rendered in watercolor.

Manufactured in China

10 9 8 7 6 5 4 3 2 1

Library of Congress Cataloging-in-Publication Data

McAllister, Angela.

[Ruby and Little Joe]

Mama and Little Joe / Angela McAllister ; illustrated by Terry Milne.—1st U.S. ed.

p. cm.

Previously published by Simon & Schuster UK in 2005, under the title: Ruby and Little Joe.

Summary: When Mama Ruby and Little Joe, two hand-me-down toys, move in with other fancy toys, they are laughed at until Little Joe finds himself in danger and the other toys band together to help.

ISBN-13: 978-1-4169-1631-4

ISBN-10: 1-4169-1631-8 (hardcover)

[1. Toys—Fiction.] I. Milne, Terry, 1964– ill. II. Title.

PZ7.M47825Mam 2007

[E]—dc22

2005029210

Mama and Little Joe

angela mcallister
illustrated by terry milne

margaret k. mcelderry books new york london toronto sydney

Mama Ruby and Little Joe arrived one day without any wrapping or ribbon.

"Which shop are you from?" asked the other toys.

"We've come from a house where the children have all grown up," said Mama Ruby shyly.

"You mean you're secondhand?" sneered Camel.

Little Joe tumbled out of Mama Ruby's pouch and somersaulted across the floor. "We're tenth-hand!" he cried with a giggle.

Camel looked down her nose at Little Joe. "You'll find everybody here is new and very fine," she said.

"Don't you get played with?" asked Little Joe.

"No. We're much too special to be played with. We get admired," replied Camel.

Little Joe whispered in Ruby's ear, "Is that the same as being loved?"

"No, dear," said Ruby sadly.

With a snort Camel walked off, and the other toys followed.

"Oh, Mama," gasped Little Joe. "I don't like it here."

"This is our home now," said Mama Ruby. "We must stay here and try to make friends."

That night Mama Ruby and Little Joe were not invited
to sleep at the end of the bed with the other toys, so
they climbed onto a bookshelf and curled up there.

Little Joe tried hard to stay out of trouble,
but he was full of bump and tumble. The toys
got cross with him every day.

Mama Ruby made herself useful, though.
She fetched dominoes for Camel.

She carried a mirror for Monkey.

She collected marbles for Polar Bear.

And she carried Mouse all
over the house.

With Mama Ruby's pouch always full, there was no
room for Little Joe. He tried riding on her tail, but he
fell off.

"You're a big boy now, Little Joe," said Mama Ruby.
"You'll have to walk."

Little Joe didn't feel like a big boy, but he pretended
for his mama. He tried to be helpful, too, but the toys
still wouldn't let Mama Ruby and Little Joe sleep at
the end of the bed.

One day Mama Ruby dropped Camel's dominoes down the stairs, and she had to go up and down again and again to fetch them. That night her legs were too tired for her to climb onto the bookshelf.

Little Joe pulled himself up onto the bed. "Please let Mama sleep here," he said. "Have a heart."

"What is a heart?" asked Mouse.

"It's what's inside you," said Little Joe awkwardly. "It's the part that cares."

"We've got the softest, most expensive stuffing inside us," said Camel. "There's nothing better than that."

"Yes, there is," whispered Little Joe to himself.

The next morning Little Joe said, "I'll carry today, Mama."

He carried marbles for Polar Bear and a doll's comb for Monkey. Then Camel called for her dominoes. Little Joe struggled to carry them all. He couldn't see where he was going, and he stepped right off the table and into the wastebasket!

Moments later the bedroom door was opened and the wastebasket was taken away.

Mama Ruby
looked everywhere
for Little Joe.
"Shouldn't we help?"
asked Mouse.
"No. It's much quieter
without him,"
scoffed Camel.

So Mama Ruby searched alone for hours in the dark house. Then, as she crept across the kitchen windowsill, she heard a cry.

"Maaaaamma!"

In the backyard, peeking out from under the garbage can lid, was Little Joe!

Mama Ruby knew she couldn't jump down that far, so she sat by the window all night and sang to Little Joe, comforting him.

The next morning Mama Ruby slipped through the open kitchen door and out into the rain.

"Mama, I can't climb down," said Little Joe.

"I'll reach you," promised Mama Ruby.

Mama Ruby climbed onto a brick, but she still couldn't reach Little Joe. She tried to push a flowerpot up to the garbage can, but it was too heavy. "If only I had some help," she sighed.

Little Joe looked up and saw the toys
watching at the window.
A tear rolled down his cheek.

Mouse gave a quiet cough. "I think . . ." he said timidly. "I think . . . I want to help."

"What?" Camel snorted. "Why would you want to get wet and dirty to help a couple of hand-me-downs?"

"I think it has something to do with heart," said Mouse.

"I'll help too," said Polar Bear.

"And me," said Monkey. "Mama Ruby helped us—now we can help her."

"Hmmmph!!" Camel huffed and puffed. "Well, of course, I am the tallest. You can't reach without me!"

So, to Mama Ruby's astonishment, Camel led the toys out to the dirty, wet garbage can. Then they climbed up onto Camel's back—first Polar Bear, then Monkey, and, last of all, Mouse.

Little Joe reached down . . . Mouse stretched up . . . and pulled Little Joe out!

"Thank you!" said Mama Ruby and Little Joe, hugging each other tight.

That night Camel made room for Mama Ruby and
Little Joe to sleep on the bed. And as all the toys nestled
together, they felt something warm inside their expensive
stuffing. Mouse knew he was feeling his heart.

"Oh, Mama, I like it here now," whispered Little Joe
as he snuggled down in Mama Ruby's pouch.

"Yes, Little Joe," said Mama Ruby with a smile. "So do I!"